Eyes
of
Stone

Dragon Riders of Osnen Book 6

RICHARD FIERCE

Dragonfire Press

Cover design by germancreative.

Cover art by Rosauro Ugang

ISBN: 978-1-947329-41-6

CONTENTS

1

"Master Anesko wants to see you in his chamber."

I looked up from the book I was reading and saw Surrel standing beside me. She was so quiet I hadn't even heard her approach. I closed the book and stood, stretching my neck and back. I'd been studying for hours and my muscles were voicing their complaints.

"Thank you," I said. "Do you know what it's about?"

"You're probably in trouble," Maren quipped from across the table. I rolled my eyes at her.

"No, sorry," Surrel replied. "It sounded important, though. And he also wanted you there." Surrel looked at Maren.

"Both of us? Now I *know* we're in trouble." Maren winked at me playfully and I couldn't help but smile.

It was nice to finally have some normalcy to life. A few months had passed since we'd restored Demris to his body and being at the Citadel with routines and sleeping in a real bed had put me at ease. Maren and I recently passed our final tests and were officially Adepts. Normally that rank would have eluded us until our fourth year, but the fall of the Conclave had caused the masters of the schools to reevaluate traditions. There was also the fact that

Maren and I had seen much more than first-year Initiates. That, more than anything, had swayed Anesko into testing us.

"Thank you," I told Surrel.

Maren stood and we left the library together. She slipped her hand into my mangled one and we walked along the halls until we reached Anesko's chamber. Since he was the new master of the school, he had taken over Master Pevus's old room. The door was wide open and I peeked inside to make sure we weren't interrupting anything. Anesko glanced up from his work.

"Come in," he bade.

I stepped into the room and sat in one of the two leather-clad seats in front of his desk. Maren took the other seat and we waited for Anesko to speak.

"How are your studies going?" he asked.

"Good," I answered.

"The same," Maren said.

"Excellent. Any word from your father?"

Maren scoffed. "You know he wants nothing to do with me. As far as he's concerned, I'm not even his daughter anymore."

"Regardless of your differences, I should think the man would at least like to know you are safe."

"Did you call us here for a reason, or just to chat?" Maren asked.

Ever since she'd invoked the Right of Secession

and been cast out of her father's court, talking about him only upset her. Anesko took the hint and sat back in his chair. He drummed the fingers of his right hand on the desk.

"Now that you have both achieved the rank of Adept, you will be given tasks that require wisdom and experience. As riders, it is our duty to patrol the kingdom and be of service to those who call upon us."

Maren and I exchanged looks. I could see the excitement in her expression, but I wasn't sure I was ready for my first official task. Granted, it was what all of our hard work and training had been for, but I had my reservations.

"You have a task for us," Maren said. It wasn't a question.

"I do. It will require more than one rider, and you two work best as a team. We're also still short of hands around here, and you two are the only ones I trust enough to be successful."

"Out with it already," Maren said excitedly. "What is it? Are we going to fight goblins in the foothills? I've heard rumors that they've been encroaching on the towns there."

"Maren, I will remind you that I am the master of this school. As such, you will keep your words respectful when you address me. Is that clear?"

That was the Anesko I remembered from my first days at the school. Disciplined, tough, formal. He was settling into his role more comfortably now, which I assumed meant he'd be less casual with us. I didn't blame him. Master Pevus's shoes would not be easily filled.

"Yes, Master Anesko," Maren answered, though she bobbed her head from side to side as she spoke. I gave her a serious look and she sighed.

"Thank you." Anesko looked down at the parchment on his desk for a moment, his eyes scanning over the words, then turned his attention back to Maren. "No, you will not be doing anything as exciting or dangerous as fighting goblins. Baron Giffor of Tiradale has requested our help. It seems his daughter has gone missing."

"He can't send his guards to find her?" Maren asked, her excitement deflating.

"The guards have been unsuccessful so far."

"How long has she been missing?" I asked.

"Two days as of his writing this letter," Anesko said. "I'm hoping this will be an easy task and that you'll find her unharmed."

"Is he sure she didn't run away?" Maren asked.

"Fairly certain. She's only ten."

"When do we leave?" I asked. If she'd been missing for two days, the trail was already cold and we hadn't even started looking.

"As soon as possible."

"I'll get our supplies together if you want to ready Sion and Demris," I said to Maren.

"Sure."

We rose from our chairs and Anesko cleared his throat.

"I'm counting on you two," he said. "We're still in the process of rebuilding our order. If we can show the people of Osnen that we're still strong, it will go a long way."

"We've got this covered," Maren replied. She left the room and I shook my head, but Anesko's lips cracked with a slight smile.

"She keeps me on my toes," I said. "But don't worry, we'll do everything we can to find the baron's daughter."

"I know you will. If I had any doubts otherwise, I wouldn't be sending you. Please make sure Maren sends me updates. I want to know when the girl is found."

"Yes, master," I said.

"One more thing. The baron asked that you use the side entrance of the castle."

I found that peculiar but I nodded. Anesko waved me off and I headed toward the kitchens to gather some food. Tiradale was only a few hours away, but I'd been so busy with my studies that I'd missed the bell for lunch. My stomach growled as if reprimanding me. After I filled a pack with food, I retrieved my sword from the armory and joined Maren in the stables beneath the Citadel.

"I can't believe our first task is so…" Maren

waved her hands around.

"Easy?" I offered.

"Boring! I want action, Eldwin. I want to fight goblins or something thrilling, not be some sort of glorified babysitter."

"Well, we aren't babysitting," I said. "In case you weren't listening, the girl is *missing*. And once we find her, we'll hand her off to her father and be back here. Maybe then Anesko will give you something 'thrilling' to do."

"Are you telling me you're fine with this?"

"I am. Honestly, I'd rather stay here and continue studying, but we will do what we must."

"That sounded so convincing," Maren laughed. "You almost had me. You're as ready to get out of here as I am."

I wasn't, but I knew arguing the point with her would be futile. Sion stepped out of her cave and I ran my right hand along her graceful neck. She'd grown by several feet since we'd been at the Citadel, but the shine of her red scales seemed duller now.

Where are we going?

We have a task from Anesko, I replied.

Sion hummed. *Good, I've been wanting to stretch my wings.*

You stretch them every day.

Yes, but it is different going somewhere else.

Flying around the Citadel grows tedious.

She sounded like Maren. They wanted to get out and do something, but I'd had enough adventures to last me for a long while. I hoped finding the baron's daughter would be easy and we could be back at the Citadel quickly. My luck in the past had never been great, but perhaps this time would be different.

I grabbed Sion's reins and led her out of the stable and into the courtyard. She staggered and almost tripped, but managed to steady herself.

What was that? I asked.

Nothing, she replied. *I'm a little clumsy today.*

I patted her neck and climbed up her shoulder and into the saddle. Maren and Demris joined us in the sunlight and I thought Demris's green scales also seemed to lack the luster they once had. Were they not getting enough nutrients?

"I'll race you there," Maren said with a mischievous grin.

"That's a bad idea," I replied.

"Why?"

"I don't want to make you cry when I win," I laughed.

"You never beat me, silly. I *always* win."

"In your dreams, maybe," I retorted, but she was right. Demris always outpaced Sion.

"Whatever. I'll see you in Tiradale."

"We'll see."

"You know what else we should see?" Maren asked.

"What?"

"The foothills where the goblins are rumored to be. Maybe we can take out a few of the nasty creatures, too."

I shook my head and braced myself as Sion launched herself into the air.

2

Maren and Demris beat Sion and I to Tiradale by half an hour.

Sion landed outside the city and I was surprised to see a new dragon stable had been erected. The last time we'd come through, Sion had been forced to find shelter on her own. I boarded Sion in the stable and found Maren waiting for me at the city gates.

"Took you long enough," she said.

"That's because I don't cheat," I replied, smirking.

"I don't cheat! How would I cheat? Demris is the faster mount."

I shrugged. "Maybe magic has something to do with it?"

Maren made a sound in her throat and punched me in the arm. "I would never use magic to beat you when I can do it on my own."

I gritted my teeth against the flare of pain and Maren smiled innocently at me. One of the guards at the gates laughed at me. I offered him a nod as we passed, but he ignored me. I expected it to feel odd being back in Tiradale. This was the place where Maren had been injured and where we'd found the map that led us to the Island of Lost Souls. Yet, as we walked the streets and headed toward the castle that towered over the rest of the city, it didn't feel odd at all.

The side entrance to the castle was guarded by soldiers wearing plate armor. Two guards stood on either side of the small gate, and they wielded halberds. As we approached, one of them stepped forward to intercept us. His insignia revealed he was a captain.

"Hail," he said. "What can I do for you?"

"We're here to see Baron Giffor," Maren replied.

"What for?"

"We're riders from the Citadel," I clarified.

"Forgive my ignorance," the captain said. He offered an awkward bow of his head, which I suspected was due to the armor restricting his movements. "Please, follow me. My lord Giffor has been waiting for your arrival."

"Forgiven," Maren said.

The captain paused as if unsure what to say, then turned to the others. "Open the gate."

One of the guards rushed to obey, struggling with a ring of keys. He managed to unlock the gate and we followed the captain across the threshold. We entered an elaborate garden and followed a loose gravel path that wound its way around statues, fountains, and shrubs that had been cut into the shapes of animals. It was beautiful, I admit, but it was all an unnecessary display of wealth. Nobles were all the same. Well, Maren was the exception. We reached the castle and the captain stopped us.

"Wait here," he said, then went inside.

I looked up at the castle and saw most of the windows were stained glass. Guards were spaced around the fortress every ten feet or so, and a thick wall surrounded the entire complex.

"It seems odd that nobody saw anything," I said, waving my hand around. "There are guards everywhere."

Maren shrugged. "Maybe they're lax in their duties and she slipped past them."

"Maybe," I agreed.

The captain returned with another man, who ushered us inside.

"My name is Osvald, Steward to Baron Giffor. I'll be in charge of taking care of you while you are guests here. Let me show you to your room."

Osvald was tall and thin. The hair atop his head was almost gone, with only the sides and back having anything to speak of. He was on the older side, as the remainder of his hair was gray and wrinkles marred his complexion. Despite his age, Osvald moved with quick steps, and Maren and I had to speed walk to keep up with him.

We reached a spiral staircase that led to the upper part of the castle and Osvald took the stairs two at a time. Maren and I struggled up after him, and I was dismayed to see Maren was faring better than me, though she was breathing heavily.

"When will we see the baron?" Maren asked breathlessly as we climbed.

"He's finishing his time with the petitions of the low borns, but he's aware that you've arrived. He'll be up shortly to meet with you."

The top of the stairway took us into a large hall. There were doors lined along the right side, all of them closed. Osvald led us to the last door and pushed it open. Maren went inside to look around while I listened to Osvald.

"This will be your quarters for the duration of your stay. I make my rounds every hour, so if you have need of anything, that would be the appropriate time to mention it. I do allow one servant to access this wing in my absence. His name is Bekim. Short, blonde. He's twelve, but he's trustworthy and can assist you if I'm not around."

Osvald spoke as fast as he walked, and it took a moment for me to digest everything he said. I nodded mutely.

"Do you need anything before I leave you?"

"I don't," I said, then looked questioningly at Maren. She shook her head.

"Very well. Please wait inside the room and don't wander the grounds until my lord has spoken with you." He offered a low bow, then turned and left. I waited until he disappeared down the stairs before stepping inside and closing the door.

"He seems high strung," Maren said.

"He's the Steward. I think that comes with the job. Besides, the baron's daughter is missing. I'm sure he's being held accountable since it happened on his watch."

"That's a fair assumption. Come over here."

Maren was standing at the room's sole window. I walked over to join her and looked out the stained glass and was afforded a magnificent view of the garden. The glass tinted it purple, but it only added to the beauty. The wall around the castle was visible as well, but the details of the city beyond were harder to make out. Maren drew close to me and I draped my arm around her shoulder. We enjoyed each other's company in silence for a while before it was interrupted.

Someone knocked on the door. Before we had the chance to turn around, the door swung open and three armed guards stepped into the room. They fanned out and a heavy-set man walked in behind them. He wore an embroidered blue tunic that was tucked into beige trousers. A flowing black cape nearly touched the floor behind him and matched the color of his polished boots. I guessed him to be in his early forties. His hair was sandy blond, cut short in the current style, and his blue eyes were sharp and calculating.

"Ah, the dragon riders have arrived," he said. "I trust Osvald ensured your comfort?"

"He did," I replied, stepping forward. The guards reflexively laid their hands on the hilts of the swords.

"Settle down, you fools," Baron Giffor reprimanded the men. "These are dragon riders, not some riff-raff off the streets. Just … go." He waved his hand toward the hall. "Get out of here."

The guards seemed hesitant to obey, but when Giffor glared at them, they hurriedly departed into the hall. Giffor closed the door and stepped further into the room.

"I apologize for their reaction," he said gruffly, one hand running over his chestnut-colored beard. "Given recent events, they're a bit overprotective."

"An understandable response," I replied. "They have every reason to be wary. Master Anesko told us your daughter went missing two days ago. What can you tell us about the night she disappeared? Who was the last person to see her?"

"Yes, that's right. Aria was in her room the last time I saw her. I tucked her in for the night and retired to my chambers. In the morning, she was gone."

"Did she seem out of sorts at all?" Maren asked.

"No. She was acting normal, by all accounts. She likes to tell me stories before she goes to bed, and that night was no different."

"Has she ever left the castle before?" I asked.

"Not by herself. She's allowed to wander within the walls and usually spends her time in the gardens. That's one of her favorite places to play."

"We'll need to question the servants and guards," Maren said. "Will they be cooperative?"

"If they aren't, I will assume they had something to do with her disappearance," Giffor replied. "All of my resources are at your disposal. Whatever you need is yours."

"It will help me to have something of Aria's, but it should be special to her."

Giffor's face lit up. "She has a stuffed bear that she carries with her everywhere. I'll have Osvald bring it to you."

"That's perfect," Maren said. "With luck and some magic, we'll have her home before dusk."

"My heart hopes that you are right."

"What does Aria look like?" I asked, knowing that was an important bit of information.

"There's a portrait of her in my chambers. I'll have Osvald bring that to you as well."

I nodded. "Is there anything else we should know before we begin our search?"

A dark look passed over Giffor's face. He opened his mouth to say something, then cast his gaze aside before he composed himself.

"Yes," he answered. "Aria isn't the first child to go missing."

3

"What do you mean?" Maren asked.

Giffor cleared his throat. "A few peasants came to me, complaining that their children had disappeared during the night."

I could see the anger burning in Maren's eyes and I spoke up before she could say anything. "How many is a few?"

"Three of four, it's not important. What's important is finding Aria."

"It *is* important," Maren snapped. "Those people may have seen or heard something that can help us. I can't believe you failed to mention that in your plea to Master Anesko."

Baron Giffor's face turned a pale shade of red and he sputtered, pointing a finger indignantly at her. "I'll remind you who you're speaking to! I'm the Baron of Tiradale! The king will hear of this affront, I promise you that!"

"Please, baron, forgive her," I said, trying to diffuse the situation. I decided to bluff. "The plight of children is one of the princess's passions."

"Princess?" Giffor's bluster vanished. "Princess Maren Toft?"

"The same," Maren replied.

"I apologize profusely," he huffed, bowing low

to her. "I heard rumors that you had become a dragon rider, but I didn't know I had the honor of hosting you."

Clearly, Maren's father had either failed to announce Maren's secession from royalty, or word hadn't traveled to the baron of Tiradale yet. Regardless, my bluff worked in our favor.

"Daylight is running short, so we should probably get to searching for Aria before nightfall," I said.

"Of course, of course," Giffor said. He gave Maren a pleading look as if asking her not to mention his offense to the king. "I will leave you to it, then. I'll have Osvald bring the items you asked for."

With that, the baron left our room. I heaved a sigh and looked at Maren. She was seething with fury, her brow furrowed.

"That pompous fool ignored the cries of help from his people simply because they're low borns? He's lucky that I *don't* hold sway in my father's court. I'd have him lashed in public!"

"I agree with you," I replied. "But it's important to remember what Anesko said. This is the start of rebuilding the people's trust in the riders. And Giffor is a noble. We both know how they are."

"That doesn't excuse his irresponsibility."

"No, it doesn't."

We stared at each other until Maren sighed and

threw herself onto the bed. It was huge, easily able to hold four people comfortably. I liked to complain about the abuse of wealth by the nobles, but I had to admit that there were benefits to luxury. I climbed onto the bed and lay on my back beside her, folding my arms behind my head.

A little while later, there was a knock at the door. This time, no one barged in. I got up and opened the door to find a young boy. He had a stuffed bear under his left arm and was struggling to hold a painting off the floor with his hands. I grabbed the top of the frame and he willingly released it.

"Come in," I said, and took the painting into the room. I set it atop the long dresser and leaned it back against the wall.

"Sorry it took me so long," the boy said. He held out Aria's toy and I accepted it, then passed it to Maren.

"That didn't seem long at all," I said. "You must be Bekim."

"At your service." He gave an awkward bow.

"We have some questions about Aria if you don't mind answering them." I stooped down so I was eye level with him. Osvald had said the boy was twelve, but he seemed short for his age. He was scrawny, too. Bekim's brown hair was long and pulled back into a ponytail, tied neatly with a white ribbon.

"I heard there were dragon riders here," Bekim

said with a huge grin. "Are you here to find her?"

"We are."

"Good. Maybe when you find her, you'll find all the other kids, too."

Maren and I exchanged looks.

"How many other kids are missing?" she asked.

"Sixteen, not counting the boy who disappeared last night. I heard about him while I was in the market earlier today."

"Sixteen?" I repeated incredulously.

Bekim nodded. "Yes, sir. Whoever is taking them doesn't care if they are boys or girls, just that they are children. But sir?"

"Yes?" I asked.

"Please don't tell anyone I told you. Steward Osvald told me to keep my mouth shut about the missing low borns because the baron doesn't want an uprising."

"I won't say anything."

"Thank you, sir. Steward Osvald also asked me to give this to you." Bekim retrieved a folded parchment from his belt and handed it over.

"What is it?" I asked.

"It has the baron's seal on it. If anyone gives you trouble or doesn't want to answer your questions, show it to them. They'll change their mind."

"Thank you, that will probably be very helpful."

"Steward Osvald told me to return as soon as I was finished here. Do you need anything else?"

"No, thank you. You've already been a big help, Bekim."

I escorted him to the door and came back to find Maren staring at the portrait of Aria. Whoever the artist was had put a great deal of detail into the work. Aria looked younger than ten in the portrait, but not by much. Her hair was the same color as the baron's, and her stuffed bear was in the portrait as well.

"We need to update Anesko," I said. "He needs to be aware of this."

"I'll tell him."

I stared at the portrait, forcing my mind to memorize what the girl looked like. Satisfied that I would be able to recognize her, I grabbed Maren's hand and gently pulled her away from the painting.

"We've got a few hours before nightfall. We should start questioning the staff."

Maren nodded and grabbed the stuffed bear from the bed. Then we left the room and began wandering the castle. We questioned everyone we came across and badgered them with questions. Most of the servants knew Aria but didn't deal with her directly. None of them had seen or heard anything the night she vanished, including the guards, and I was starting to grow worried that the trail was too cold.

"She likes to play in the gardens, mainly the large one by the side gate," a maid had told us. It matched what the baron had said, and Maren and I decided to search that area first. We walked along the loose gravel paths, peering into bushes and looking for any signs that Aria may have left the walkway. There were no visible clues. No errant footsteps, no damaged plants, nothing.

It's almost as if she were taken by magic, I mused, sending my thoughts to Sion. *But Maren said there's no residual spell energy, so that doesn't seem to be the answer.*

Sion hummed in reply, the sound filling the bond.

Perhaps she was taken by a winged beast? That would answer why there are no footprints.

I don't think so, I replied. *There are no signs of a scuffle. In fact, there's no evidence to suggest she was even out here that day.*

Maren and I were passing a stone bench and we stopped to take a break. I sat down and rubbed my forehead in frustration. The sun was beginning to set, and a servant was lighting the lampposts that were scattered throughout the garden.

I smell something, Sion said.

Probably another dragon, I replied.

No. The smell is coming through the bond. It's a heavy earthen smell, like fresh dirt.

I glanced around. There were bushes, flowers,

and other growing things outside of the pathways, but none of them appeared to be newly planted.

I don't see anything, I said, but I kept looking around.

"What is it?" Maren asked.

"Sion smells fresh dirt through the bond. Do you see anything?"

We both left the bench and stepped off the pathway, pushing through the bushes. My right foot unexpectedly dropped into a hole in the ground and I fell.

"Are you all right?" Maren asked.

"I think so," I replied. "I just hurt my pride a little."

She laughed. I had hurt my leg, too, but it wasn't bad. I crawled backward out of the shrubbery and parted it with my hands, peering at the ground. There was a hole where my foot had fallen through, but there was also a much larger hole next to it.

"You might want to see this," I said, raising my voice so Maren could hear me.

"Don't tell me you broke your leg," she replied. "I don't want to see that."

"Just get over here."

I heard the crunch of her footsteps as she approached, then she crashed through the bush and stopped beside me.

"You *did* break your leg, didn't you? I told you I didn't want to see it. You're going to have to crawl back to the castle because I'm not carrying you."

I rolled my eyes at her.

"Get down here and look," I grunted.

Maren got down on all four beside me and looked at the ground.

"Your foot isn't that big," she said.

"Yeah, I know. That's not a hole," I replied. "It's a tunnel."

4

"Let's see where it goes," Maren said.

"Should we let the baron know first? Maybe he can send some of his guards with us."

"I think the less he knows, the better. He didn't want to do anything to help the other children. Let him worry about Aria for a while. Maybe it'll teach him some compassion."

When Maren made up her mind about something, I knew it was impossible to sway her. I shrugged and moved aside so she could lead the way. The tunnel was roughly two feet wide and three feet high, which meant we were forced to crawl. As we traversed the passageway, I lost all sight in the darkness. Maren stopped at one point and my head collided with her backside.

"Get your butt out of my face," I grunted, backing up.

"Get your face out of my butt," Maren replied. "Hold on, I think I hear something."

I held my breath and listened. Water was dripping somewhere ahead of us.

"Can you see anything?" I asked. "I'd hate to drop off a ledge into an underground river or something."

"I wanted to conserve my energy, but you make a good point."

Maren conjured a ball of light and it illuminated the darkness. She continued along the tunnel and stopped again a short distance later.

"Guess where the tunnel leads?" she asked.

A foul odor assaulted my nostrils and I gagged.

"The sewers," I groaned.

"How could you tell?" She laughed. "There's a ladder here. I'm going down."

I crawled forward to the edge and glanced around the sewer while she descended. A stream of sickly green water flowed along the ground and the odor intensified. I didn't want to breathe through my nose, but I also didn't want anything getting into my mouth, so I decided to suffer through the stench.

"There's a walkway down here." Maren's voice echoed oddly off the walls. "Though it doesn't look like anyone has been here in a while."

I grabbed ahold of the ladder and made my way to the bottom. The sewer was a fairly simple design. The walls were made of brick and cemented with mortar. Aside from the walkway, which was cobblestone, the floor where the water ran was dirt. Or mud. Or any number of other unimaginable things. The stream of gross water was only a few inches deep and ran eastward. At least, I think that was the track it took. My sense of direction was thrown off.

The cobblestone path was dirty, and a pile of old bones was strewn about haphazardly. I couldn't tell if they were human or not, but given their apparent age, I doubted there were any threats nearby. Still, I kept my hand on the hilt of my sword. Dirt from the tunnel above had collected along the scabbard and I absently brushed it off. Thin trails of moss snaked along the walls, making it appear as though there were long cracks in the brickwork.

"I don't see any manholes," Maren said, guiding her magical sphere of light around the ceiling of the tunnel.

"If I had to guess, I would say this filth runs away from the castle. And if that's correct, then there should be entrances further down. How far do you think it goes?"

"Only one way to find out." Maren smiled.

I groaned inwardly and followed her further into the sewer system. For most of the way, there was just the main tunnel. Occasionally, smaller tunnels branched off, but we didn't want to risk getting lost. We kept to the main waterway until Sion spoke through the bond.

Be careful. I sense something foul.

Too late for that, I replied. I tried to project a complete image of our surroundings to her, but all I got across was my feeling of disgust and a smattering of glass-like fractures of the water's image.

Why do humans pool their foul matter into the ground? She snorted in disdain.

So that it's not out in the open like dragons tend to do. I flooded the bond with my mirth, but Sion wasn't impressed. *You said it's something foul. Can you tell what it is?*

Not quite. The scent has a hint of something familiar, but it's difficult to place. It's something ... serpentine.

A dragon?

No. Sion's certainty was unmistakable.

"There's something in the air that Sion doesn't like," I said to Maren.

"Demris just told me the same thing."

"Great." I drew my sword and took the lead. Other than the occasional rat and the constant flow of water, there was nothing out of the ordinary. I kept my guard up and trod slowly, making sure there were no surprises. It felt like an eternity before we encountered the first manhole.

"There," Maren said, pushing past me. She tucked the head of the stuffed bear under her belt and climbed up a set of bricks that stood out from the wall. I watched her struggle briefly to push the steel grate off, then she climbed out. A moment later, her head appeared over the hole.

"We're in the city," she said.

I sheathed my blade and climbed out of the sewer, then slid the grate back into place. The fresh air was a welcome reprieve and I exhaled through my nose, trying to get rid of the stench.

"Let's not do *that* again," I muttered, then looked around. We were in an alley. The buildings around us were tall enough that the narrow backstreet was entirely shaded.

"At least we didn't have to walk in the water," Maren said. "It could have been worse."

She was right, as usual. It certainly could have been worse. "Where are we?"

We walked to the end of the alley and Maren stepped out onto the main street. A crowd of people had gathered near a vendor cart where an old woman was selling charms of protection. The people were clamoring to get her wares, some of them asking for two or more of the trinkets.

"Are those actually powered by magic?" I asked.

"No. She's a charlatan."

It was a despicable trade, but it wasn't illegal. The buildings along the street were the usual spots. A metalworker's forge, two taverns, a weaver's shop. I scanned the storefronts but didn't see anything suspicious.

"Maybe Aria didn't come out through this manhole," I suggested.

"Maybe," Maren said, her attention focused on the woman peddling fake protection.

"Do you want to go over there and stop her?"

"Hm? No. I'm more curious about her customers. Why is there such a demand?"

Maren crossed the street and stood behind the crowd. I occupied myself by walking along the street. The castle grounds weren't far from here, which would make for an easy escape if someone had taken Aria. The general atmosphere of the area was one of hesitance. People glanced at me suspiciously as they hurried about their business. And I noticed something else.

There were no children present.

I glanced at Maren and saw she was still waiting in line, so I entered the building beside the alley we'd exited. It was a bakery. The smell of fresh bread filled the place and I closed my eyes and inhaled a deep breath, which aided in clearing the lingering stench of the sewer still in my nose.

"Be with you in a moment," a man's voice called out.

There wasn't much bread left on the counter, but that wasn't a surprise with the quick approach of nightfall. A man came in from the back of the shop, carrying a tray with rolls that glistened with melted butter. He set the tray down and wiped his hands on his flour-covered apron.

"I'm all out for the evening. Someone's purchased this lot," he added. "And these rolls are for me."

"No worries, friend," I replied. "I'm not a customer, anyway. I'm looking for a child, a girl. She's blond, about this tall," I held my hand out beside my hip. "Have you seen anyone with that description?"

The baker shook his head slowly. "I'm afraid

not. There's been lots of them going missing lately, but I haven't seen any of them. It's a sad state of affairs, to be sure."

"Do you have any of your own?"

"Nah. My wife's barren. I've always seen it as a curse, but now I'm thinking it might be a blessing. I don't know how those parents are making it through the day, much less the night. That's when they go missing."

"So I've heard," I said. "Do you ever work late into the evening?"

"Not usually. I try to be home for dinner."

I nodded, glancing around the shop. "I'll be around if you see anything, or you can send a message to the castle. Just tell them to deliver it to the dragon riders."

"Riders, you say? I didn't know there were any in town, but I don't have much time to gossip. Bread doesn't bake itself, you know."

"One more question, if you don't mind?"

"Sure, anything if it helps."

"Do you know when this all started? The baron seems less … knowledgeable … about the daily lives of his subjects."

The baker squinted and rubbed his chin. "I think a couple of weeks ago. That's when I first heard anything."

Seventeen children over a few weeks. I was beginning to get the feeling something darker was going on in Tiradale.

"Thank you."

I turned to leave and as I reached the door, the baker said, "Actually, there's something else. Something odd I heard yesterday."

5

I released the door handle and turned around to look at the baker.

"My apologies," he said. "Like bread, my thoughts rise slowly sometimes. I just remembered something that I heard yesterday. One of my customers mentioned that a family who had a child disappear found a statue on their doorstep a few days later."

"A statue?"

"Aye, a statue. Said it looked just like their missing child, down to the birthmark on his left cheek."

"Why would someone leave a statue?" I spoke the thought aloud without realizing it.

"Who's to say? That just popped into my mind and I figured you'd like to know."

"Unfortunately, it only adds to my questions, but thank you. Please let me know if anything else comes to mind."

"I will. Stay safe out there."

I stepped out of the bakery and saw Maren was talking to the old lady at the cart. Her crowd was gone and the street was practically empty. I glanced at the setting sun. It would be dark within an hour. I strode over to Maren and caught the last bit of the old woman's words.

"They fear what's hunting their children in the dark," she said. "I don't blame them, and you shouldn't, either."

"I don't blame them," Maren replied, glancing over at me. "I just want to get to the bottom of this. If you know anything, tell us."

"If I knew anything, I would have reported it to the guards. I need to get home before dark if you don't mind."

Maren waved her off and I watched her push the cart along the street until she turned onto a side path. "What was that about?"

"She's profiting on the fear of parents who are concerned about their children. Those charms are nothing but plain rocks, but she's selling them to people with the falsehood that they'll keep the children safe."

"When the people find out she's tricked them, she'll have to answer to the mob of parents she duped. That's her problem."

Maren nodded.

"I spoke to the baker in that shop over there. He told me something strange. A statue showed up at the house of one of the missing children. Stranger still, it looked just like the child."

"That is very strange," Maren agreed.

"Why do you think someone would do that? To honor their loss, maybe?"

"I suppose that's possible." She untucked the

stuffed bear from her belt and held it up. "It's time to use magic."

Maren closed her eyes and began whispering strange words. Despite the numerous times I'd been around magic and seen its effects, I was always awed by it. When I had learned that some riders gained magical abilities from the bond with their dragon, a part of me had hoped I would gain them. So far, that had yet to happen. Maren completed the spell and a faint glowing line stretched out from the bear.

"This should lead us to Aria."

We followed the main street until the glow turned left, taking us down a thoroughfare with ramshackle homes. Candles burned in most of the windows, and I saw the face of a young boy curiously staring out one of them. His mother pulled him away and peered out at us. I offered a wave, but she quickly covered the window with a sheet.

Maren was focused on her spell, so I kept quiet and followed beside her, occasionally watching the shadows when I thought I saw movement. Whether it was my eyes playing tricks on me or scurrying creatures, nothing moved while I watched. Darkness eventually fell over the city, but we continued following the trail by the light of the moon. The sky was cloudless, and the moon was large and bright, illuminating the street enough that we didn't need a torch.

The glowing line led us down various streets, through neighborhoods and past closed shops, and there seemed to be no end in sight. The time slipped away and as we continued our trek, I began to notice that people had gone to bed. Homes were dark and silent. My feet were beginning to ache, but I tried to ignore the discomfort. Somewhere out here, Aria was alone and likely scared. I consoled myself with the knowledge that she was probably with the other missing children, but what could a child do against whatever, or whoever, had taken them?

At some point, I noticed that our surroundings looked familiar. A few shops lined the road and the castle was back in our line of view. I looked at Maren, but she was still engrossed in her spellcasting. Her eyes were drooping and her pace had slowed considerably. The light took us to the left again, and I realized we were back where we began. I spun around, eyeing the buildings. The bakery, the weaver's shop ... we *were* back where we'd started.

"Stop."

Maren continued walking and I had to grab her arm to break her trance. The glowing line faded from existence and she blinked several times, looking at me confusedly. Her eyes were red from exhaustion.

"We just went in a huge circle," I said.

"Oh." She looked at the bear in her hands, then at our surroundings. It took her a moment to get her bearings, and then she frowned.

"Why didn't the spell lead us to Aria?"

"I'm not sure," she replied. "It should have. Unless…"

"Unless what?"

Maren looked me in the eyes, her expression worried. "Unless she's dead."

I refused to let that be an option. "No, she's not. If she was, then why would your spell have worked? Why would it have started tracking someone who isn't here?"

"You're right," Maren said. "It couldn't." She smiled sheepishly. "It could be me. I got tired and was just putting one foot in front of the other."

"We should get back to the castle. We'll get some rest and try again in the morning."

Maren was shaking her head before I finished speaking.

"No. She's already been missing for two days. I can't stomach leaving her out here for a third."

I was tired, but the idea of a helpless child out here somewhere helped give me a second wind of energy.

"All right," I conceded. "Let's try again."

Maren offered a weary smile and repeated her spell. Just as before, the glowing line flowed along the main street and we began the search anew. I tried to remain more alert this time, and I was constantly checking on Maren to make sure she wasn't too tired to continue. She was more awake now and there was purpose in her steps.

As far as I could tell, the magic was leading us along the same route as before. We passed a pair of guards who stopped us, but when I presented the baron's letter, they let us go. Aside from the guards, we didn't see another living soul until we passed through a housing district. All of the homes looked the same, so it was difficult to tell if we'd come through the area already.

Maren nudged me, driving her elbow into my side. It didn't hurt, but the surprise caused me to make a noise that sounded like a chicken being strangled. I snapped my gaze at her and she pointed off to the side. I looked, but there was nothing there. No, I was wrong. A woman was sitting on the ground in front of her home. She blended in with the shadows and I was impressed Maren had spotted her at all.

We slowed as we neared the dwelling and the woman looked up. The moon was still our primary source of light, but the glowing line helped reveal the terror on her face. She scampered back on all fours and bumped into the door of her home.

"It's all right," Maren said. "We aren't going to hurt you."

"Who are you?" the woman asked.

"We're dragon riders."

"Why are you out this late?" She was still pressed up against the door and her demeanor hinted that she didn't believe Maren.

"I'm sorry if we startled you. We're searching

for the baron's missing daughter."

"His daughter was taken, too? Oh, gods, no one is safe!"

"Why aren't you inside?" Maren asked.

"I was, but I heard something and when I opened my door, this statue was here."

The statue was beside the door and hidden in the shadows. I would never have seen it if the woman hadn't mentioned it. Even with the moon shining brightly overhead, the darkness was impenetrable in some spots. I drew my sword and surveyed the area.

"Did you see anyone?" I asked.

"No."

Maren walked closer and the glowing line illuminated the shadows. The statue was short like a child, and when the light revealed the face of it, the woman gasped. I spun around, prepared to find some terror of the night behind us.

"It's my boy," the woman said. She began sobbing and wrapped her arms around the statue. Maren and I exchanged glances.

"It looks like your son?" Maren asked.

"To the detail," the woman answered. She released the statue and turned to us. Tears ran down her cheeks. "A friend of mine also received one. Her daughter went missing a few days before my son did."

I sheathed my blade and leaned in close to look at the sculpture. It was highly detailed. I didn't know much about the practice of sculpting, but I knew it was time-consuming. The fact that someone had crafted such a detailed piece told me that whoever had left the statue must have seen the child. And that meant it could be the person responsible for the disappearances.

"We should keep going," I said to Maren. "And you should get back inside. I'll have some guards check on you in the morning. If you see anything, let them know."

The woman wiped her face on her sleeve and nodded sadly. "I hope you find the monster responsible."

"We will," I vowed.

Maren and I left the woman behind and followed the glowing line until, once again, we ended up outside the bakery.

"I don't understand," Maren said. "The spell is working. I can feel the magic pulling the bear toward *something,* but we keep ending up back here."

"You know, this feels familiar," I said. "It's almost like when we were trying to find the dragon Assembly in that forest."

"That's it!" Maren said excitedly.

"What?"

She closed her eyes and I waited impatiently. Finally, she opened her eyes. "I can't sense it, so it must be well hidden by someone *very* powerful, but it's the only explanation."

We stared at each other for a moment, and at the same time we both said, "Magic."

6

I started to think that we were in over our heads. If Maren couldn't detect the magic confusing her spell, then it was someone powerful indeed.

"It's late and we're not making any progress. Let's go back to the castle and regroup. You'll need to tell Anesko what you've discovered and see what he wants us to do, anyway."

The defiance that had been in Maren's eyes earlier was gone and she nodded tiredly. I put my arm on her shoulder and we walked together back to the castle. The main gates were barred and the guards wouldn't even acknowledge us, so we followed the wall to the side entrance. The shift had changed and the soldiers there weren't the same ones we'd dealt with earlier.

One was sitting on the ground with his back against the wall, half asleep. The other was using his spear as a prop of support as he slouched. I intentionally cleared my throat loudly enough that they could hear it. The soldier on his feet straightened and whipped his head toward us so quickly that his helmet almost came off. He lifted the spear and pointed the end at us.

"Hey! You aren't allowed here."

I pulled the baron's letter out and held it up. "We're guests of Baron Giffor."

The soldier eyed me suspiciously but eased

forward to grab the letter. His eyes scanned the parchment, then he grunted and handed it back.

"Any luck in finding his daughter?"

"Not yet," I replied.

He grunted again and turned around, kicking the other guard awake. "Keys, Dwayne."

Dwayne pulled his ring of keys out and tossed them up. The other guard scrambled to catch them but they slipped through his fingers and fell on the ground with a loud rattle. He scowled at Dwayne and kicked him again, harder this time.

"Bah, just pick them up, you fool!"

"Don't throw them next time." The guard bent down and retrieved the keys, then unlocked the gate and pushed it open.

Maren and I went through and the gate and it clanged shut behind us. The voices of the guards carried into the garden. They were still arguing about the keys. Maren drew close to me and grabbed my hand, entwining her fingers with mine. Although she had given up her claim to her father's court, it was still hard to believe that a princess, *the* princess, had chosen me.

She has good taste in character, Sion said.

I smiled. The longer Sion and I were bonded, the more our thoughts easily drifted into each other's minds.

I think there's a sorcerer behind the disappearances, but Maren isn't able to sense their magic.

There was a moment of silence.

Yes, I can feel it. Sion confirmed. *When I try to focus on the source, it slips away and leads me in circles.*

That was worrisome. Dragons were highly magical creatures. For something to elude Sion, it had to be trouble. And why was this mysterious person expending so much energy to hide Aria and the other children? There were too many questions and I was starting to get a headache.

"What was that?" Maren asked.

"What?"

"I thought I heard something, but maybe I'm just tired."

We stopped moving. Ahead of us, I could hear footsteps crunching on the loose gravel. Peering with squinted eyes, I spotted a shadowy figure. I drew my sword and sprinted toward them.

"Stop!" I shouted.

The figure looked back at me, then turned and fled. I ran as fast as I could, trying not to lose the person in the maze-like garden. The figure left the path and dove into some bushes. I cursed under my breath and followed after them, but when I crashed through the shrubbery, the person was gone.

I smell it again, Sion said. *The scent from the sewers. Be careful!*

I stabbed my sword into the bushes, but all my

blade hit was branches and leaves. Maren came jogging up.

"Where did they go?"

"I don't know," I replied. "It's like they vanished into the air."

"Or the ground," Maren said, kneeling. "The tunnel is here. They must have escaped into it."

The adrenaline pumping through me faded quickly, leaving me breathless. I sheathed my sword and kicked at the ground in frustration.

"That had to be the person behind all this," I said. "Who else would know about the tunnel?"

"I think you're right. Do you want to follow him? Or her? Whoever they are."

We stared at each other in silence. My sense of duty told me to go in after them, but my body begged for rest and sleep.

"No," I finally answered. "I can barely think straight. It would be easy to walk into a trap."

Maren surprised me by nodding in agreement. "We'll find them tomorrow."

I hoped that would be the case, but I didn't want to get my hopes up. We left the garden and entered the castle, quietly traversing the stairs and finding our room after getting turned around. The pale moonlight filtered in through the stained glass, bathing everything in a multicolored glow.

"I'm going to try and reach Anesko," Maren said. "I know it's late, but he's usually up around this time."

I stripped my boots off and climbed onto the bed, falling asleep almost immediately. The dream I found myself in was odd. I was chasing the shadowy figure and followed them into the sewer. A snake-like creature attacked me, ripping into my flesh as I watched helplessly. I awoke with a start, drenched in sweat, my heart racing.

Maren was lying next to me. She rolled over and muttered something in her sleep. I sat up and rubbed my eyes, looking to the window. It was still dark out. My throat was parched and I left the bed, pouring myself some water from a pitcher that sat on the dresser near the painting of Aria. I stared at it as I drank, my mind still fuzzy with sleep.

I downed the rest of the water and walked over to the window. Clouds had filled the sky and darkness covered the landscape. Something moved in the garden, but when I focused my attention on it, there was nothing. Had it been my imagination, or was it the figure from earlier? I watched a while longer but saw nothing else. Chalking it up to my sleepiness, I went back to bed.

A noise awoke me and I opened my eyes. Someone was knocking on the door. I looked at Maren. She was still out. I forced myself off the bed and opened the door. It was Osvald. He had a troubled look on his face. He glanced down the hall, then back at me, and spoke lowly.

"May I have a word with you?"

"Of course," I replied, stepping aside to let him

in. He strode inside and I closed the door. "What's going on?"

"It's Bekim. He's missing."

"Missing? What do you mean?"

Osvald's hand trembled as he ran it across his face. "He was running late to my chambers, which is unlike him. I waited as long as I could, then started my normal errands. When he still hadn't shown up, I went to his room. He wasn't there."

"That doesn't mean he's missing," I said. "Where else does he go?"

"Nowhere," Osvald said, shaking his head. "I-I'm afraid that he …"

As my mind slowly became alert, I remembered that I'd seen movement in the garden earlier. My heart sunk into my stomach as I realized that may have been Bekim being taken.

"Calm down," I said, as much for his sake as for mine. "Maren and I will be back out in the city today looking for Aria. We'll also look for Bekim. I'm sure he's fine. He seems resourceful."

The steward looked like he was on the brink of tears. "I apologize," he said. "It's just that I had no idea anything was happening in the city until Aria disappeared. The baron told me about the disappearances after she was gone and made me swear to keep quiet about everything. I fear that may have been the wrong course of action."

"I have to agree. The baron will have more

trouble on his hands than he likes if we don't stop whoever is taking the children. I'll wake Maren and we'll start searching again. Can you prepare something quick to eat?" I was hungry, but I also thought the man could use a task to keep himself from thinking about Bekim.

Osvald nodded. "Yes. Do you need anything else?"

"Not yet. Have you seen the baron this morning?"

"Yes. He asked if there were any updates about Aria. That was before I realized Bekim was missing."

"If you see him again before we do, you don't know anything. Let us speak to him."

"As you say," Osvald replied.

He left the room and I turned to the bed. Maren was awake, watching me.

"We should have told the baron about the tunnel, shouldn't we?" she asked.

I couldn't help but think the same thing.

7

"What bothers me the most is how this person is taking the children," Maren said as we made our way down the castle stairs. "Take Bekim. If he was in the castle, how did this person get past all the guards and *inside* the castle, find Bekim's room, and then sneak off with him? It just doesn't make any sense."

"I've been wondering the same thing and, so far, I've got nothing. The only explanation would be magic, but …" I shrugged. "Speaking of, were you able to get word to Anesko?"

"No," Maren replied. "I tried reaching him, but something was interfering with the magic."

I was convinced the interference had something to do with this mysterious figure stealing children. I'd been refraining from saying anything, but I couldn't keep my mouth shut anymore.

"I think we need help," I said.

Maren gave me a look that said she thought I was insane. I patted the air with my mangled hand.

"You can't sense the magic keeping us from tracking Aria, right? Sion said she can feel it, but it slips away when she tries to find its source. That tells me whoever this sorcerer is, he's more powerful than us, even with our dragons. Doesn't that worry you at all?"

Maren had been a rebellious rulebreaker when we first met, and she still was. She also didn't like to think herself incapable of anything, which had led to more than a few problems. Despite her carefree attitude, I knew that she was smart and cunning. She might play the role of a confident sorcerer, but she knew her limits. It just helped for me to remind her of them sometimes.

"Maybe a little," she smirked. "Come on, Eldwin. We've faced worse things than a slippery sorcerer."

As we reached the bottom of the stairs and turned the corner, we nearly ran into the baron.

"My apologies," I said, stepping to the side and waving him on.

"I was just coming to find you," Giffor said. "Have you found anything yet?"

"Not yet," Maren quickly replied. "We searched the city late into the night, but we didn't find anything helpful."

"It seems that dragon riders are not as proficient as the rumors claim." Giffor folded his arms over his chest, resting them on his plump stomach.

His words ignited my anger, and I had to grit my teeth to keep from saying anything. Maren, on the other hand, didn't bother with decorum.

"*You* asked for *our* help," she said. "It would have been appreciated if you could've at least shared all of the relevant information with us before sending us off to blindly search for Aria."

"What do you mean? I told you everything I knew."

"Please," Maren said tersely. "Don't think us fools. You knew very well there were more than just three or four children missing. There's almost twenty!"

"That doesn't matter!" Giffor raised his voice to a shout. "What matters is that you find Aria. Are you telling me that you've found *nothing at all?*"

"No," Maren replied calmly.

Giffor scowled and turned to me.

"No," I lied.

"Then how did you enter into the sewers?"

Maren and I exchanged looks.

"Now who's a fool? I have spies everywhere. Yes, I know about the tunnel in the garden. And I also know that Bekim is missing. And yes, I also know about *you*." Giffor turned his imperious gaze on Maren. "You're no more a princess than I am."

I felt a lump form in my throat and swallowed.

"You have one more day to find Aria, or I'll inform the king about your little indiscretion. And I'll let your master at the Citadel know, too."

Before either of us could say anything, the baron pushed past us and stormed down the hall. A moment later, Osvald came rushing by.

"I'm sorry!" he hissed, shaking his head. He handed a small bag to me. "I tried!"

I offered him a smile, hoping he knew I didn't have any hard feelings toward him. Maren looked at me, her eyes full of fire.

"Let's go."

We left the castle and ate quickly, devouring the fresh bread and cheese that Osvald had placed in the bag, then we entered the garden. Maren stomped all the way to the tunnel. A single guard was there. He wore a bored expression and straightened his posture when he saw us.

"We're going in there," I said.

"If you must," he replied. "There's a terrible stench coming out of that hole."

"That's because it leads to the sewer."

The guard scrunched his nose in disgust.

"Ladies first," I said to Maren.

She shrugged and summoned a ball of light, then entered the tunnel. I nodded at the guard and crawled in after her. We made it to the sewer and climbed down the ladder. There was evidence that the figure from last night had come through here. Muddy boot prints lined the cobblestone pathway, leading toward the city.

"I wonder how the baron found out about you," I said.

"Who knows? It doesn't matter, though. I don't want trouble with my father, so we need to find Aria." We walked in silence for a moment before she asked, "When you said we needed help, what were you thinking?"

"We need eyes up high, so I was thinking you could have Demris fly over the city while we search. It would be a good idea to bring Sion into the city using the collar, too."

"I thought you were going to suggest getting the baron's soldiers involved."

"That's probably also a good idea, but we can use his letter to commandeer soldiers without dealing with Giffor directly."

Maren sideways glanced at me, a smile pulling at her lips. "You're starting to think like me. I like it."

We reached the manhole we'd used the day before and found the footprints ended at the ladder, making it clear that the figure exited the sewer from here. We climbed up the ladder into the alley and Maren pointed into the sky. I looked up and spotted Demris's sleek green body gliding overhead.

"I told him to leave the stable on his own. He had to growl at the attendant. The man wet his pants before letting him out," Maren giggled.

"They're not going to like boarding him anymore," I said with a smile. "Does he see anything that doesn't look right?"

"Let's see."

Maren's eyes rolled into the back of her head until only the whites were visible. It looked so unnatural, and I had to turn away and blink rapidly to keep my eyes from watering. She'd recently learned to share Demris's vision, but it was creepy.

"I don't see any magic being used," she said. "Well, except for me." She turned her head from side to side slowly. "Wait. I see something on the eastern side of the city."

"Magic?" I asked.

"No, but there's a scent in the air coming from there. Demris doesn't know what it is, but it doesn't fit in with the other smells of the city. It's a building next to an arena of some sort, but there are no people. It seems abandoned."

"Sounds like the perfect place to hide."

"I agree. We should check it out." Maren's green irises slowly slid back into their normal place and she blinked. "Hopefully you can learn to do that with Sion. It's one thing to see things from up high on Demris's back, but it's a completely different experience seeing things through his eyes."

"I'm going to get Sion," I replied, trying not to be jealous of her newfound power. "Are you coming?"

"No, I'll stay here. I want to keep an eye on this manhole just in case someone comes in or out."

"All right. I'll be back."

I left the alley and followed the streets to the main entrance, then turned left and reached the stable. Sion was waiting, her eagerness flooding the bond. Her saddle hung on the wall inside the stall, and I retrieved the collar and a plain robe from it.

"You ready?" I asked, rubbing the scales on her neck.

Yes.

I put the collar on and watched as her body shrank and changed until she was in her human form. I handed her the robe and she covered her nakedness, then we went back into the city. As we walked along the street, Sion lifted her head and sniffed the air.

Do you smell it? I asked. *That scent you mentioned?*

Yes. It's strongest here in the city.

Maren found an abandoned area to the east, and we think it's coming from there. She's waiting for us near the market district.

I led Sion along the streets and noticed that she was moving slower than normal. I paused to let her catch up. She seemed winded, which wasn't like her.

"Are you all right?"

Yes ... but I'm having trouble focusing.

I put my hand on her shoulder and saw her forehead was glistening with sweat. Her skin had gone pale. Was something in the city affecting her?

I'm feeling light, Sion said, her voice weak. And then she collapsed.

8

"Sion?"

I knelt beside her and shook her shoulder. She was unresponsive. Fear constricted my throat and I looked around. A few people had stopped to stare. I wanted to ask for help, but what could these people do to help a dragon?

Sion?

Still nothing. Her mind was blank like an empty dark cave. I lifted her into my arms and turned back the way we'd come. She'd been fine outside the city. It must be that smell she kept talking about. Or perhaps it was the magic from the mysterious figure. Panic was starting to take over. I stumbled and almost dropped Sion. My arm muscles were burning from the exertion and I stopped to adjust her position over my shoulder.

I received a few odd stares, but I ignored them and continued carrying her out of the city. I took her back to the stable and set her down in the stall. Maren was waiting for me, but I couldn't leave Sion. I ran my fingers along the side of her face, tucking a few stray red hairs behind her ear.

It felt like an eternity before I felt her presence through the bond again, but it had probably only been a few minutes.

"Sion," I whispered. "Are you hurt?"

No. She lifted her head weakly and looked around. *Where are we?*

"We're back in the stable. You passed out on the street." I sent a swirl of partial images through the bond.

I don't know what happened. My legs grew tired and my body was hot, and then everything went dark.

"Was it the smell? Did it overpower your senses?"

It wasn't the scent. It was merely a moment of weakness. I feel fine now. Let's go.

"No," I said, shaking my head. "I think something in the city caused it. You need to stay here."

Sion attempted to sit up, but her human body didn't cooperate. She fell back down.

Don't look at me like that.

"Like what?"

Like I'm dying. I'm not.

"I know that. I'm just worried about you."

Don't be. Go.

"I can't leave you right now."

Sion closed her eyes and growled. It sounded much less intimidating from a human body.

I'm fine. Go find the girl.

"If anything happens to you ..."

GO!

Her command was so strong through the bond that I fell backward as if she had physically shoved me. I rose to my feet and reached down for the collar, but Sion feebly slapped at my hand. I left it on her and hurried out of the stall. It tore at my heart to leave her so vulnerable, but she swore she was fine. I knew without any doubt it had something to do with the person taking children. I was going to find them, no matter what it took.

I pushed through the crowds of people packing the streets and swiftly returned to where I'd left Maren. She wasn't in the alley. I figured she'd probably got tired of waiting on me, so I stepped back onto the street and looked around. The old woman with the cart of fake charms was back, but I didn't see Maren.

Suddenly, Demris bellowed overhead.

His roar echoed off the buildings around me and I had to cover my ears against the noise. He swooped around, flying urgent circles over the city. The people around me cried out in fear, pointing at Demris.

Sion?

I'm here.

Any idea what's going on with Demris? He's acting erratically.

I'm not sure, Sion replied. *He's in pain, but he doesn't have any wounds. And he says he lost Maren.*

I looked into the sky and watched Demris slowly spiral down until he landed outside the eastern side of the city.

How did he lose Maren?

He doesn't know. He says he can't fly right now, but I don't know why. His thoughts are an incoherent mess.

"Great," I muttered. Something was affecting our dragons, and Maren had apparently wandered off somewhere. I doubted she would have gone to investigate alone. I decided to wait for her to return. I paced the alley, occasionally glancing through the metal grate into the sewer, but there was nothing except darkness and foul smells.

The minutes passed uneventfully and turned into an hour. Then two. I looked for her in the crowds that passed, but there was no sign of her. The baker came out of his shop and offered me a roll, which I enthusiastically devoured. I licked the remnants of butter from my fingers and headed back to the castle. Perhaps Maren had returned there looking for me.

I entered our room, but there was nothing out of place. If she had returned at any point, it was impossible to tell. I decided to go back to the city. Osvald was coming out of one of the other rooms and I waved him down.

"Have you seen Maren?" I asked.

"Not since this morning. Is everything in order?"

"I think so …" I paused, an idea coming to me. "Can you do me a favor?"

"I can't lie to the baron," Osvald said, his eyes going wide.

"You don't have to. I need a few soldiers, preferably ones with experience."

"I know just the ones," the steward replied. "Should I direct them to meet you somewhere?"

"I'll wait for them outside, near the side entrance to the garden."

"Very well. I'll go and get them now."

A short while later, three soldiers came trudging along the path. I didn't recognize any of them until one lifted the visor of his helmet. It was the captain from the first day we'd arrived, the one who'd brought us to Osvald.

"My lord," he greeted, lowering his head.

"Please, call me Eldwin," I replied. "There's no need for formalities."

"I'm Gregor." He motioned to the others. "This is Crispin and Kennet, my right hands."

I nodded at them and looked at Gregor. "What can you tell me about the arena on the eastern side of Tiradale? Does anyone use it?"

"It used to be for games of sport before the new arena was built. It's been neglected since, as far as I know."

"I think Aria is there," I said.

Gregor's face lit up. "The baron will be glad to have her back."

"As will I, but we need to use caution. I'm certain there's a sorcerer behind her kidnapping. Maren is a sorcerer, but unfortunately, I can't seem to find her." Once the words left my mouth, it fully hit me. Maren had probably been waylaid by surprise while she waited in the alley.

Has Demris heard from Maren? I asked Sion.

A pause.

No. He's still trying to get his bearings, but he can feel her presence in the bond.

At least she was conscious. That was a good sign. I was probably overthinking things, but I decided to expect the worst and hope for the best.

Gregor stared at me expectantly.

"Sorry, I was speaking with my dragon. Are there any places around the arena with a view of things, but where we can remain hidden?"

"There's a few," Gregor replied.

"Good. I want us all at different vantage points so we can watch for anything unusual. Is there a signal you use to communicate with each other?"

"Sure." Gregor wet his lips with his tongue and issued a soft whistle that sounded like a bird chirping.

"That works for me. Show me where these hiding spots are."

I followed Gregor's lead and we left the garden through the side gate. The arena was on the eastern side of Tiradale, built right up against the walls that protected the city. The closer we got to it, the fewer people we encountered. A couple of homeless people were sleeping against some of the abandoned buildings, but otherwise, the area was empty.

Crispin entered one of the buildings, a two-story brick structure with broken windows. He went to the top level and stood near one of the windows. Kennet climbed atop a small hovel on the opposite side of the street. A glance inside revealed that it had once been used as living quarters by someone.

Gregor and I continued around to the opposite side of the arena. A ladder behind a dilapidated shop gave me access to the roof, and Gregor took up a position atop a similar building crosswise from me. Between the four of us, we formed a squarish outline around the arena. Now that I saw it, the arena was more of a circular list field, surrounded by long benches made of stone that tiered upward, offering seating for a few hundred people. A wooden gate provided entrance to the field.

We're at the arena, I told Sion. *Do you sense anything?*

Magic, she replied. *Lots of it. I'm trying to determine what the spells are, but it's difficult.*

How's Demris?

I think he's resting. He seems to be asleep.

At least he wasn't threatening to tear the city apart to find Maren. I looked up at the sky and guessed it was shortly past noon. The sun was bright and hot, but dark clouds were on the horizon, a promise of coming rain. I sat still and watched, not sure what I was looking for. After a while, I started to doze in the heat. I tilted my head from side to side, cracking my neck.

Down below, near the wooden gate, I spotted movement. A robed figure came into view. I leaned closer to the edge of the roof, peering intently. Was that the person we were looking for? I looked to where Gregor was positioned, but he must have been lying down because I couldn't see him. A faint melody drifted on the air, but I wasn't sure where it was coming from.

Something creaked behind me and I turned to look, just in time to see Bekim swinging a staff at me.

Pain exploded along the left side of my face and then everything went dark.

9

When I came to, my head was pounding.

I was in the arena, propped up against the lowest level of stone benches, my arms bound behind my back. I struggled against the bonds, but the rope was tightly secured in place. It was evening now, and a light rain was starting to fall. Torches burned at random intervals around the list field, but they did little to illuminate the darkness. The flames sputtered and hissed against the wind and rain.

You're awake, Sion's voice filled my mind, easing the ache a little. *Now I know where you are. I'm on my way to you.*

"I thought you were dead," Crispin whispered from behind me.

I jumped, startled, and looked over my shoulder. He and Kennet were sitting on the bench above me, also bound, but there was no sign of Gregor. Another form was slumped across the bench beside them. In the flickering torchlight, I recognized Maren's red hair.

"Maren!"

"Ssh," Crispin hushed, nodding toward the field. "He doesn't like noise."

"Who doesn't?" I looked to where he'd indicated and spotted Bekim. The boy was dragging a statue roughly his height toward a wagon.

"What's he doing?"

"I'm not sure, but he's under some sort of spell. I think it has something to do with that music."

I could hear the faint notes he was talking about. I'd heard them earlier, too. Just before Bekim had struck me. I watched the boy as he struggled to lift the statue into the wagon. He succeeded after a few tries, then he marched back across the field, disappearing into the thick shadows.

"Where's Gregor?"

"We haven't seen him," Crispin replied.

A hissing noise filled the air, followed by a terrified scream. And then silence.

"What was that?" I whispered.

"I don't know, but that's the fourth time I've heard it."

Bekim came back into view again, dragging another statue. A bright flash of lightning lit up the arena momentarily. At the far end of the field, I spotted something that looked like a mix between a dragon and a snake. It was long, probably ten feet in length, with four legs and a tail that had a wicked-looking barb on the end. It was covered in scales, but unlike a dragon, the scales weren't flat and smooth. They were rough and jagged, with thick spikes rising from their centers. Its neck was abnormally long, flowing in a U-shape like a snake poised to strike.

The darkness seemed more intense when the

light faded, leaving the image of the creature burned into my mind's eye.

"Gods," Crispin said. "What was that thing?"

I tried to show the image to Sion through the bond, but it went through in fragmented pieces. I was determined to master the ability no matter how many failures I experienced. One of the fragments was of the creature's head, and I could feel the bond flood with Sion's revulsion.

Do you know what it is? I asked.

Yes. It's a basilisk. They are dangerous creatures.

What's a basilisk? Is it like a dragon?

No! Sion's revulsion doubled in intensity. *Such a mindless thing is not even close. You must not meet its gaze, or you'll be turned to stone.*

Stone? I watched Bekim lift the second statue into the wagon, and realization dawned on me. The missing children were being turned into stone. I tried to wriggle my hands free of the rope again. The material cut into my wrists, and I felt blood trickle down my palms. Other than causing myself pain, I was making no progress with getting free.

"The woman is awake," Crispin said.

I looked back to see Maren sit up. Her hands were bound, but she was also gagged. Our eyes met and she tried speaking, but the words were muffled in the cloth and came out as gibberish.

"Sion is on her way, but she's in human form," I

said. "Can you reach Demris?"

I watched her facial expression go from curiosity to worry. She shook her head.

"Sion said he was sleeping earlier," I said. "Don't worry about him right now. He's safe, but we're not. The creature over there is a basilisk. Whatever you do, don't look it in the eyes."

"Why not?" Crispin asked, horror evident in his voice.

"Because you'll turn to stone."

Kennet had been strangely quiet, and it occurred to me that I hadn't heard him speak at all since I'd met him.

"What's with him?" I asked, nodding to Kennet.

"He lost his tongue in a poisoning incident."

"Oh. I'm sorry."

Kennet didn't seem bothered by my question. He lifted his right leg and wiggled his foot around. He mouthed something I couldn't make out, but Crispin smiled.

"That's brilliant. He's got a dagger in his boot. Let me turn around and I'll try to pull your boot off."

I turned back to the field to make sure nobody saw what they were doing. Bekim was gone. The music still hung in the air, the tune a haunting melody.

"Got it," Crispin said. I heard the dagger clatter

onto the stone. "Hold still while I cut through your rope."

Kennet was freed and he stepped down beside me, then hurried to a pile of weapons I hadn't noticed. I saw my sword was there among the pile, too. Crispin started working on my bonds, but I pulled away.

"Maren first," I said, turning to face him.

He began cutting the rope around her hands and Kennet returned, setting my sword at my feet. Then he cut me free with his blade. Crispin was the last to be unbound.

"We need to get out of here," he said.

"We can't leave Bekim," I replied, staring at the dark field. "And what about the basilisk? It poses a danger to the entire city."

"There's only four of us. That's not enough to take down that creature. And what about the sorcerer?"

"Let me worry about him," Maren said.

"Did you see him?" I asked.

She nodded. "I heard something in the sewer while I was waiting on you. When I went down to check it out, he got the better of me. He won't do it again."

"We need a plan."

"There's no time for plans," Maren argued. "I'll find the sorcerer. You guys deal with the basilisk and the other guy."

"What other guy?" I asked.

"There's another man with the sorcerer. From what I could gather, they're working together but the sorcerer isn't the mastermind."

"Always more surprises," I muttered. "Let's try to find this other man, but stay clear of the basilisk. Sion should be able to take care of it when she gets here."

How far away are you? I asked her.

I'm not sure, but I'm close. I can practically taste the basilisk's stench. Vulgar creatures.

Maren climbed up the benches until she reached the top tier, then she sprinted around the arena, disappearing into the darkness. I buckled my sword onto my waist and led Crispin and Kennet to the wagon. A dozen statues were inside, but there was no driver. No horses were tied to the wagon, either.

I heard footsteps and motioned the other two to get down. We huddled near the front of the wagon, and I watched Bekim come into view, dragging another statue.

"It's just the boy," Crispin whispered. "We can take him."

I shot him an incredulous look. "We're not killing an innocent child."

"Of course not," he replied. "We just need to immobilize him."

"Yes, but how?"

Kennet suddenly bolted around the cart and

grabbed hold of Bekim. Crispin shrugged and joined the man. Bekim struggled like a wild animal until he unexpectedly went limp in their arms. I noticed the music had stopped. Maren must have found the sorcerer. There was a shout of alarm, but it hadn't come from Crispin or Kennet. Something was coming our way, something big.

The basilisk.

The creature raced into view, its brown body undulating back and forth like a running lizard. It headed straight for the wagon. Kennet rushed forward to meet the creature, bringing his sword up. He leaped, but before he could strike, the basilisk weaved its head down and met Kennet's gaze. The soldier's limbs froze in place, a gray tint spreading from his head down. His stone body continued sailing through the air for a moment, then crashed at the feet of the basilisk and shattered.

I watched in terror, unable to move or look away. Fear had me ensorcelled as if I, too, had become stone. The basilisk stopped to sniff Kennet's remains, then set its gaze on Crispin. Thankfully, the man had lowered his head, refusing to look at the beast. That small victory mattered little as the basilisk drew closer to him and Bekim. The boy was still motionless.

My mind screamed at me to do something, anything. The rain was falling harder now, thick drops drenching my hair, small rivulets of water running down my face. I pushed through my fear and was able to clench my fingers around the hilt of my sword. I drew my blade out of the scabbard slowly, but the basilisk must have heard it.

Its head swiveled up from Crispin and looked directly at me.

10

I snapped my eyes shut and lifted my blade horizontally to help block my face, praying it was lined up correctly and when I peeked out, I saw my own eyes reflected in the metal. Relief washed over me, but it was short-lived as I heard the basilisk scrambling toward me. In the metal, I saw movement behind me.

Sion!

Get this collar off me, she growled.

I spun around as she drew closer and awkwardly removed the collar with my good hand, then ducked back behind the wagon and dropped the collar. Sion started to shift back into her dragon form, but the change was slow and lethargic. Something was still affecting her, but she stumbled toward the basilisk anyway. The two massive creatures collided just as Sion's transformation finished. They rolled around violently, jaws snapping and claws slashing at each other.

Crispin carried Bekim to where I was and we hurried across the field to the wooden gate. I sheathed my sword and pushed the gate open far enough for him to squeeze through with the boy, then turned to go back.

"Where are you going?" Crispin asked.

"I have to help Maren," I replied. "Get the boy to safety. If you see Gregor, tell him to keep anyone from coming in here." I turned and sprinted back to the benches, scrambling up the tiers until I reached the top. I went the same direction Maren had and crouched down when I heard a roar. Something huge flew overhead and swooped down into the arena.

It was Demris.

Finally, something in our favor. The green dragon joined the fray, digging his claws into the back of the basilisk. He flapped his powerful wings, stirring up dust and debris from the field, and pulled the basilisk away from Sion. The dragons were longer and thicker, but the basilisk was quicker. It broke free of Demris's grasp and dodged left and right, avoiding the dragons' powerful talons. A cry of pain broke my focus on the dragons.

It was Maren.

I ran ahead, following the curve of the arena until I spotted her. She was struggling to her feet and had something in her hand. I reached her and wrapped her in a tight hug, thankful she was safe. A thin line of blood seeped from her nose.

"I failed," Maren said.

"What happened?"

"The sorcerer got away. I was so close to stopping him, but I got this." She held up a flute, but it wasn't like anything I'd ever seen before. It was white and had runes etched all along its surface. "It's what he was using to control Bekim."

"At least he won't be able to lure children out of

their homes now. He'll go into hiding if he knows what's good for him."

"We still have to deal with the ringleader," Maren said. "He cursed the sorcerer as a coward and ran down to the field."

I couldn't see the dragons or the basilisk from here, but their fighting echoed across the arena.

"Demris is helping Sion," I said.

"I know. When he woke, I told him we needed his help. He sounded different somehow."

"Sion has been acting off, too. I think it has something to do with that flute."

Something crashed below. Maren and I hurried down the tiers and into the field. Near the wall was a line of statues, most of them children. I paused when I passed a taller one and realized it was Gregor. His mouth was open in a silent scream. I pulled my sword from the scabbard and stalked around the other statues. I paused behind a large shipping crate at the end of the line.

There was another crash and someone cursed. I peered around the corner of the crate and saw a man standing at a makeshift desk, shoving gold coins into a large leather bag. He wore finely tailored clothes, expensive items I would have expected to see on a noble. The number of coins he was shoveling into the bag was a small fortune. Had he been selling the statues? I stepped into the open and pointed my blade at him.

"What are you doing?" I demanded.

The man whirled around, spilling some of the coins from the bag. He saw my sword first, then looked at me.

"Who are you?"

"I'm Eldwin Baines of the Dragon Guard," I said. "I'm apprehending you for murder, by order of the baron of Tiradale."

"Murder? I haven't murdered anyone."

"That's your basilisk, isn't it? Where's the baron's daughter?" I desperately hoped she was still alive. Maren stepped beside me, staring death at the man.

He shifted his gaze between Maren and I and looked like he was about to run, so I stepped closer and jabbed the tip of my sword against his chest. His bravado faded and he lifted a quivering hand to point behind me.

"She's over there."

I didn't dare turn around, but I heard Maren step away and, a moment later, she confirmed what he said. "It's her. Aria's h-here." Her voice cracked on the last word, sending a stab of pain into my heart. I thrust my sword forward, pushing the man against the desk until he was practically lying on it.

"Why?" That was all I could get out without breaking, but it was all I needed to say.

The man stuttered over his response, cursing the sorcerer who'd abandoned him before saying, "Money."

"Who did you sell these statues—these *people*—to?"

"You'll never know," the man spat, becoming rebellious again.

Maren laid her hand on my shoulder. I glanced at her briefly. She nodded, and I knew we were both thinking the same thing. I handed Maren my sword and grabbed the man by his shirt, jerking him roughly to his feet. He tried to resist, but Maren poked him in the back with the blade and he stopped. I pulled him further into the field, toward the sounds of fighting.

I've got something for the basilisk, I told Sion. *The man responsible.*

I'm a bit busy, she huffed.

Once we were within the range of the basilisk, I shoved the man in front of the creature. Sion leaped aside, dodging a swipe from the basilisk's claws, and accidentally whipped the man's leg with her tail. His leg bent in two, clearly broken, and he dropped to one knee with a scream of agony. Sion shielded Maren and me with her body while Demris hunched low, preparing to launch himself at the basilisk.

I ducked down to see beneath Sion's belly. The man continued to howl in pain, but he must have recognized the bigger danger he was in. He rose and tried to shamble away, but the basilisk's head snaked back and forth between Demris and the fleeing man. Seeing the easier prey, it scrambled after the man and slapped him to the ground with its right claw.

Demris remained crouched, waiting. The man begged for his life, making all sorts of promises to the basilisk as if it could understand him. The creature seemed amused at first, watching the man struggle under its claw. It tilted its head to the side curiously, then stared intently at the man. He must have had his eyes closed because he didn't turn into stone. The creature made a chortling sound, then raised its claw just high enough to stab one of its talons into the man's shoulder.

He screamed and must have opened his eyes, for the same gray tint slowly spread across his body, silencing his screams forever. I suddenly felt sick. Had this been the wrong decision? Should we have taken him to the baron and let him pronounce judgment on the man? Possibly. Instead, we'd sentenced him to death at the hands of the very creature he'd used to kill innocent children. I struggled with my sense of right and wrong, but ultimately, I knew that justice had been served. It was a fitting punishment for the crime, but who was I to enact that punishment?

You did what was just given the circumstances, Sion said. Her words eased my doubt somewhat, but I had the suspicion that Master Anesko probably wouldn't agree.

The man's entire body turned to stone, then the creature stomped on him, crushing him into a multitude of pieces. Demris wasted no time. He leaped forward, snapping his powerful jaws around the basilisk's neck, jerking from side to side. His brute strength lifted the basilisk off the ground, but the basilisk's body undulated with the movement and it broke free of Demris's mouth. Sion charged ahead, but the basilisk retreated, dodging and weaving away from the dragons.

I need to rest, Sion said. *The creature is swift, and I grow tired again.*

Now that she'd said something, she did seem sluggish. She snarled and snapped at the basilisk, but it evaded her and struck her in the chest with its barbed tail. Sion's scales protected her from harm, but she staggered back from the force of the blow.

"We have to do something," I said, looking at Maren.

"I have an idea."

11

Maren stuffed the flute into her boot. It was too long, though, and it stuck out awkwardly like a bone.

"Tell Sion to move away."

"Are you sure?" I asked worriedly.

"Yes. I'm going to trap the basilisk with a spell, but if Sion or Demris are near it, it'll trap them also."

Get out of there, I told Sion.

She turned about and swung her tail at the basilisk, but her aim was off, and the creature easily dodged it. Sion leaped into the air, but her wings barely kept her off the ground. She landed back on the field with a loud thud. The basilisk turned to engage Demris, which allowed Sion to put some distance between them.

"Get ready," Maren said. "I'm about to send Demris away next."

I gripped the hilt of my sword tightly and hoped Maren knew what she was doing. Demris lowered his head and charged the basilisk, managing to get the bulk of his head under its stomach, then he jerked his head up, flipping the basilisk into the air. It landed on its back and Demris withdrew.

Maren ran closer, lifting her hands and chanting words of magic. The air around the struggling basilisk started to ripple and a humming sound filled my ears. I didn't like the idea of Maren being so close to the creature and I hurried after her. She stopped roughly ten feet away and closed her eyes, chanting the same phrase over and over. The rippling air solidified into glowing walls.

The basilisk flipped itself back onto its feet and sprinted toward Maren. I stepped in front of her and braced myself, but the creature slammed into the barrier and was kept at bay. The basilisk roared and tried again. The barrier held, which put the basilisk into a frenzy. It began wildly swinging its tail, clawing and biting at the walls, all to no avail. Maren had stopped chanting, but her face was strained.

"It's … failing," she gasped.

"How?" I looked from her to the barrier. It flickered under the onslaught of the basilisk, but it was still holding. For now.

"There's something wrong with the magic," Maren said. She groaned and her expression turned to one of pain.

To make matters worse, Sion's presence in the bond was weakening. I looked to where she was and saw her lying on her side. She was breathing, but it was slow like she was asleep. It was all too much. I felt cornered and helpless. I checked to see if Demris was being affected. He was crouched nearby, his breathing ragged, but he was on his feet.

Maren cried out and fell to her knees. The barrier withered and disappeared, freeing the basilisk. It screeched triumphantly and shot toward us with blinding speed. Without thinking, I lifted my sword and stepped in front of Maren to shield her.

Time seemed to slow.

Thick chunks of mud and grass were kicked up into the air as the creature hurtled straight for us. I heard Maren curse behind me. Somewhere in the distance, crickets chirped their nighttime tune. Thunder cracked overhead, and everything sped up. The basilisk was going to kill us, I had no doubt of that.

And then something in the bond tickled my mind. It was a foreign feeling, but it reminded me of my test at the Citadel when I had been given a potion that allowed me to cast spells. I let the energy flow into my mind, and euphoria coursed through my entire body. I felt powerful, strengthened. And I saw a vision of a mirror forming, expanding off my sword.

Except it wasn't a vision.

The energy coming through the bond was streaming out of my hand and onto my blade. The mirror looked like it was made of water, and it extended until it was as long as I was tall. The basilisk skidded to a halt and issued a roar of challenge. I barely understood what was happening. How was magic coming through the bond? And why? I felt for Sion's presence. She was there, but she was buried behind the coursing flow of magic. The basilisk roared again.

I instinctively turned to look, remembering at the last moment not to meet its gaze, but it was too late. I found myself staring into the face of the basilisk. I gasped and knew that my time was up. The seconds ticked by, and I was still alive. And then I saw the gray tint spreading from the basilisk's eyes, spilling out like paint covering a canvas. The mouth of the creature froze in place and it stopped breathing.

The basilisk had turned itself into stone.

Maren pushed me aside and the mirror spell shattered like crystal, a thousand faceted pieces fading from existence. I dropped my sword to the ground and felt the magic evaporate from the bond.

"How did you do that?" Maren said, turning to face me.

"I-I don't know," I stuttered. "It just … happened."

"You were glowing like a star. I thought I was seeing things, or that I had died, but it was real. You did it, Eldwin! You cast your first spell!"

My confusion gave way to elation. My bond with Sion had finally produced magic! But something was wrong with her. Her presence was shrinking somehow. Was she—

"Sion!" I screamed. I ran to her but tripped and fell. I crawled the rest of the way, scraping my palms on the ground in my rush. I ignored the pain and reached her face, wrapping my arms around her.

"What's happening?" Maren asked as she knelt beside Sion. She placed a hand on Sion's scaled chest and closed her eyes. After a moment, she shook her head. "I can't feel my magic. We need to get her out of here."

"How? She's too big. Demris doesn't seem to be faring well, either."

"Where's the collar?" Maren asked.

I'd forgotten about it. "It's by the wagon," I replied.

Maren rushed away to retrieve it. She came jogging back a moment later and handed it to me. I put it around Sion's neck. She shifted with an agonizing slowness than felt like an eternity. Finally, her human form lay naked on the ground. I picked her up and carried her out of the arena.

"I'll meet you at the stable," Maren called out.

I didn't have the words or the strength to reply. I carried Sion along the empty streets, navigating my way toward where I thought the gates were. My mind was a scattered mess and I wasn't even sure I was going the right way. Somehow, I made it to the main street. I passed a tavern as the door swung open, and music and laughter spilled out into the street.

Almost there, I told myself, pushing my muscles to their limit. For some reason, I felt like if I could just get her to the stable, everything would be fine. By the time I passed through the gates, I was gasping for breath and my legs felt like melted butter. They gave out on me before I reached the stable, and I collapsed. My entire body was drenched in sweat.

I lied there, unable to move for a long while. Eventually, the burning in my muscles subsided and I was able to push myself onto my knees. Sion was still, but her chest moved up and down with a steady rhythm of breathing.

"Sion?" I whispered. My throat was parched and I barely recognized my own voice.

Her head lolled to the side and her eyes cracked open.

"Thank the gods. Are you all right?"

You worry too much, she replied. *It takes more than fatigue to kill a dragon.*

I laughed in relief despite the tears that escaped my eyes. "I was scared you were dying this time. Are you ill? Why are you so weak?"

Sion remained silent for a moment, then said, *I'm not sure. My body doesn't ache, but there is something wrong.*

"Demris is also being affected," I said. "You both need to stay out of the city. Something there must be causing this."

I don't sense anything from the city, but perhaps you are right.

I stood and helped Sion to her feet. We supported each other the rest of the way to the stable, then I removed her collar. She returned to her dragon form faster this time, and she stretched out in her stall and closed her eyes. I sat beside her for a few hours, watching over her as she rested. She seemed in better health away from the city. Perhaps the sorcerer who'd escaped was responsible. His magic had controlled Bekim, and possibly others, so it only made sense that he was able to do something harmful to Sion and Demris.

I caught myself dozing and stood up. Footsteps outside the stall drew my attention and I peered out. It was Maren.

"How is she?"

"She's resting," I replied. "What about Demris?"

"The same," she answered. She hesitated like she had more to say.

"What is it?"

"Giffor wants to see us."

<h1 style="text-align:center">12</h1>

We strode back to the castle in silence. I noticed Maren had removed the flute from her boot and stuck it into her waistband. It was so pallid, it appeared to glow ominously, standing in stark contrast to her clothing.

Although the rain had stopped, the streets were slick and partially flooded in some spots. We passed a group of soldiers on patrol. Showing them the baron's letter kept them from trying to detain us, but a few drunks had the misfortune of getting belligerent with them and received an armed escort home. Once we reached the castle grounds, things were quiet.

We navigated our way along the garden path and, as the silence stretched, I couldn't stop thinking about Aria and the other children, and how we had failed to save them in time. Granted, most of them had been taken before we ever got word of it, but I still felt burdened by it.

I was exhausted and wanted nothing more than to crawl into bed and sleep for a week. Once we entered the castle, we were greeted by servants rushing around, some of them wiping sleep from their eyes as they went about their tasks. I exchanged glances with Maren.

"There you are! Thank the gods."

It was Crispin. Osvald was with him and they

converged on us, both trying to speak at once. Crispin quieted and let the steward talk.

"Baron Giffor is awaiting your presence in his personal chambers. I'll take you there."

We fell into step behind him. Servants dodged around us as we traversed the halls. Finally, we entered a wing of the castle I had not seen yet. There were more soldiers standing guard here than anywhere else. An oak door banded in steel was at the end of the hall, and Osvald pushed it open and ushered us in. Crispin waited outside and the steward closed the door behind us.

The room we entered was well lit with candles. A large elegant desk was the centerpiece, and a thick plush white rug covered the majority of the stone floor. There were other items, too. A half-empty bookshelf, various animal heads mounted on the walls, and a rack of swords that looked unused.

Baron Giffor entered the room from a door to the right. Before it shut, I saw it was his sleeping quarters. He was alert despite the late hour and seemed pleased with our presence.

"You've found her?" It sounded more like a statement than a question.

"Yes," I answered after side-eyeing Maren.

"Where is she?"

"She's in the old arena." I couldn't bring myself to tell him of her fate.

"Is she with Gregor? Why didn't you bring her

to the castle with you?"

"She's been turned to stone," Maren interjected. "Along with Gregor and many others."

The baron's face went pale. He glanced toward his bed-chamber, then back at us, and lowered his voice. I guessed the baroness was sleeping, or perhaps he didn't want her to hear the news yet.

"Who is responsible? I'll have them hanged from the castle gates."

"There were two men involved," Maren replied. "One of them met his death at the hands of a basilisk. He was using the creature to turn children into stone, and we believe he was selling them. The other was a sorcerer who escaped."

"Escaped? You mean he's walking free in my city?"

Maren shook her head. "I don't know that for certain, but it's probably a safe assumption."

Giffor chewed on his lower lip, then looked at Osvald. "I want every available guard on the streets. Now. No one rests until he's found."

Osvald offered a bow and left the room. Giffor narrowed his gaze on Maren.

"You're a sorcerer. How do you reverse this?"

"I can't." Maren's shoulders subtly slumped, and I knew she felt as burdened as I did.

"What do you mean? Are you telling me …?" Giffor trailed off and his eyes grew watery. The realization was setting in.

"I'm afraid so, my Lord," I said. "There's nothing we can do."

"Yes, there is."

Bekim stepped ahead of us and bowed to the baron. "While I was under the sorcerer's spell, I couldn't control my own body, but I could see and hear everything. It was like being trapped inside my own head." His fingers fiddled with the edges of his sleeves, which were too long for his arms. "The two men talked about how the people who were turned to stone might become alive again. The sorcerer told the other man there was no need to worry about that because there was only one way for that to happen and it required a special potion."

"What kind of potion?" Maren asked.

Bekim shrugged. "I don't know. He didn't say the name of it or anything."

"We need to find the sorcerer," Maren said, looking at me.

I nodded.

"Yes, you two better find him. If my daughter is lost, I'll have you both thrown in the dungeon."

"It's likely Aria was already turned to stone before you summoned our aid," Maren said. "And unless you want your castle demolished by two angry dragons, I wouldn't advise putting us in your dungeon."

"Speaking of your dragons, where are they? Why haven't they found the sorcerer?"

"They're … indisposed," Maren said vaguely.

"Something in the city is making them sick," I added. "We think it has to do with the sorcerer's magic."

"Useless creatures. I want you two out there with my soldiers. Find that sorcerer and get me that potion." He stalked across the room and returned to his bed-chamber.

I looked at Maren. Her eyes held the tiredness that I felt. I expected her to rebel against the baron's command, but instead, she nodded resolutely.

"We need to find him before he leaves the city if he hasn't already. If there's any chance that he wasn't lying, that potion will save all those lives."

"I'm with you," I said.

Bekim led us back out to the main part of the castle. If I'd thought it was chaotic before, it was pure insanity now. Soldiers were streaming from every area of the castle and forming into groups. An older man with a gray handlebar mustache was issuing orders and assigning the groups to specific sections of the city.

"I want to try tracking the sorcerer with this," Maren said, pulling the flute from her waistband and holding it up.

"Do you think it'll work? If he was using magic to hide Aria before, I'm certain he's using the same spell to hide himself now."

"Yes, that does worry me, but maybe your new

magical power will help with that."

"I'm not even sure how it works, but I can try."

Maren handed me the flute and I closed my eyes and focused on the bond. Sion was still resting, but her presence felt stronger now. That was a good sign. I searched the bond for the energy I'd felt before, but there was no trace of it. I opened my eyes and looked at Maren.

"I've got nothing," I said, heaving a sigh. I'd hoped that I had really unlocked magic with the bond, but the mirror spell must have been a fluke.

"It's all right," Maren replied. "You don't become a master with one try." She whispered slithery sounding words and waited, but nothing happened. The blue glowing line didn't appear like it had when we searched for Aria, and Maren frowned.

"When I cast the spell against the basilisk, the magic was coming from the bond. I don't know if Sion was channeling it or not, but it was definitely coming through our connection. I don't know if that makes any sense, but maybe you can do the same thing with Demris."

"That's interesting," Maren said. "Dragons are highly magical creatures, and that's why some riders can use magic, but it's usually minor spells. What you did wasn't something easily done." She pursed her lips and held the flute up, eyeing it closely. "It's worth a try."

Maren inhaled a deep breath and kept her eyes

on the flute. She spoke the words to the spell again, and this time, the glowing line formed.

"That was genius," Maren smiled at me.

"Well, that *is* why you like me, isn't it? For my cleverness?"

Maren scoffed and started following the magical trail. It took us away from the castle and into the city. I expected that it would take us back to the area near the arena. It would make sense that the sorcerer would want to remain out of sight, and since the area was abandoned, that would be the logical place to hide out.

And I was wrong.

The spell led us to an inn near the main gates of the city. We went inside and found a few people enjoying ale near a blazing fireplace. A serving girl was wiping tables with a dirty cloth and she smiled tiredly at us.

"We're about to close," she said.

Maren ignored the girl and headed for the stairs that led up to the rooms.

"Keep them down here," I said, motioning to the people near the fire.

The girl was clearly confused, but there was no time to explain. I followed Maren up the stairs. The glowing line stopped at the door to a room on the left. I quietly drew my sword. Maren ended the tracking spell and summoned a barrier shield around us. We looked at one another and nodded.

I kicked the door open.

13

A wave of heat crashed over me as I stepped inside the room.

Maren's shield deflected the flames that erupted down from the doorway, and I threw myself to the ground on instinct, dropping my sword. I should have expected a trap. Booted feet ran past me, then there was a thud and a cry of surprise. I stood up and saw a robed figure sprawled on the floor. Maren pushed past me, palm outstretched, and uttered a spell. Thick webbing shot from her hand, pinning the sorcerer down. It reminded me of a spider web, only the cords were fatter and silver in color.

"Hiding in plain sight," Maren said. "Clever."

"Impossible," the man cursed. "How did you find me?" He struggled to free himself, but the webbing didn't budge. There was something odd about his voice.

Maren knelt beside him and covered his mouth with her hand, then glanced back at me. "Hand me something to gag him with."

I glanced around, but there wasn't much in the room. I retrieved my sword and cut a swath off the sheet from the bed, then handed it to her. She balled the material up and stuffed it into the sorcerer's mouth. He managed to spit it out and Maren covered his mouth again.

"If you try to utter a spell, it will be the end for

you. Understand?"

The sorcerer nodded his head. His face was hidden by the hood of his robes, but as he nodded, it fell back to reveal his features. The man was young. He had to be the same age as Maren and I, if not younger. Maren held the flute in front of his face.

"You were using this to control people. What is it?" she asked. She hesitantly removed her hand from his mouth.

"It's funny that being a dragon rider, you've never seen a dragon's bone before."

"Where did you get it?"

"I made it," the sorcerer replied.

"Lie to me again," Maren said. "I dare you."

"Threaten me all you want. I'm not afraid of you."

"Bekim said you mentioned a potion that can reverse the effect of the basilisk's stare. What kind of potion?"

"Who's Bekim?"

"The boy you spirited away from the castle." Maren glowered.

"Oh, him. His name is Bekim, is it?"

I stepped forward and jabbed the tip of my blade against his knee. "He doesn't need both legs, does he?"

The sorcerer glared at me. I hoped he didn't call my bluff, because I really didn't want to cut his leg off. I tried to keep an imposing look on my face, but I wasn't sure if it was working.

"If he doesn't tell me about the potion, I'll let you cut them both off."

Maren's tone was serious. I hoped she didn't call my bluff, either. Perhaps I'd made an error in speaking up.

"It's an elixir," he answered.

"Made of what?"

"I have the recipe in my spellbook. It's in the drawer." He looked at the side table beside the bed.

Maren nodded at me and I removed my sword and checked the drawer. A red leather-bound book was inside. I grabbed it and handed it to Maren. She covered the sorcerer's mouth and awkwardly thumbed through the book.

"It's here," she said.

Relief washed over me. There was still hope. Maren scanned over the list of ingredients and looked up at me.

"Cut him free," she said. "We'll take him to the castle and let the baron do as he pleases."

I wasn't sure how she planned to keep the sorcerer secured while we took him there, but I shrugged and hacked through the cords. It took more effort than I expected, and by the time he was free, I had worked up a sweat.

Maren gagged him again, and this time he didn't spit the cloth out. She took my sword and cut more strips from the sheet while I kept an eye on him. She handed the sword back to me and tied the sorcerer's hands behind his back. The expression on her face suggested that she was enjoying herself. He'd done the same thing to her, so I couldn't fault her for it.

We escorted the sorcerer out of the room and down the stairs. The serving girl had finished cleaning the tables and the people who had been drinking by the fireplace were gone. Their unfinished drinks were sitting on the floor, and I suspected that they had hightailed it out of the inn when they'd heard the noise.

"Sorry about the sheet," I said, fishing a coin from my purse and handing it to her. "That should cover the cost, but if not, tell your boss to take it up with the baron."

The girl nodded, wide-eyed and nervous. Her hands trembled at her sides. I smiled comfortingly and we left the place behind. The trek back to the castle was uneventful. I'd expected trouble from the sorcerer, but he didn't fight or try to escape. That worried me a little, but when we handed him off to the guards at the castle, I pushed the apprehension away.

"I'm going to speak with Giffor," Maren said. "I'll meet you up in the room."

"Do you want me to come with you?" I asked.

She shook her head. "No. Go get some rest. You look like you're about to fall asleep on your feet."

I didn't argue with her. I went to our room and was asleep almost as soon as my head touched the pillow. I awoke lying in the same position I'd fallen asleep in, my boots still on. I don't think I'd moved all night. My vision was bleary and I was still tired, but the light of dawn was shining through the window, forcing me into wakefulness. I reached for Maren, but she wasn't there.

"Maren?"

I sat up and looked around. Her side of the bed didn't appear to have been slept in. My first thought was that something had happened, but I quickly discounted the idea. Someone would have alerted me. At least, I hoped someone would have. I reached out to Sion. Her presence was strong and she greeted me with a pleasant hum.

Goat, she said. *It's delicious.*

Is that what they're feeding you?

Yes. Another hum.

Have you seen Maren?

Not since last night. Why?

She's not here, I said. *She was supposed to meet me back at our room.*

There was a long pause. *Demris said she's at the arena with the statues.*

I whispered a silent thanks to no one in particular and washed my face with the water from the pitcher on the dresser. With any luck, we'd be heading back to the Citadel today and wouldn't need it anyway. I left the room and spotted Osvald coming up the stairs. I walked toward him, meeting him halfway.

"The baron has asked for an update," the steward said.

"Tell him we'll get back to him. Maren never came to bed, so I'm going to see what's going on."

"Very well, I'll pass your message along to him. I also wanted to thank you."

"For what?" I asked.

"For rescuing Bekim. I think of him as a son, and when he went missing, I didn't know what I'd do if he never came back."

"It isn't just me who deserves credit," I said. "Crispin got him to safety, and Kennet gave his life. Gregor ..." I paused, not sure what to say. He'd been turned to stone, but now that we had the recipe for the potion, I held hope he'd be restored along with all the others. I'd learned long ago that hope was a fickle mistress, but every once in a while, she managed to surprise me. Perhaps now would be one of those times.

"I've already organized a memorial service for Kennet. I'm waiting until we know whether the potion works for the others ..." he trailed off.

I patted him on the shoulder. "You're a good man, Osvald. I'm going to find Maren. I'll return as soon as I can."

"Do you want breakfast before you go?"

My stomach rumbled as if replying to him, but I shook my head. There were more important things than breakfast right now. "I'm fine."

I went down the stairs and entered the garden, taking the side gate since it was closer to the arena. Several guards were blocking access to the street that led to the arena, but they let me through when I showed them the baron's letter. I reached the entrance to the arena and slipped through the wooden gate, which was partially ajar.

The entire place looked completely different during the day. The ground of the list field bore the damage from the previous night. The dirt held long claw marks everywhere, and in a few spots, large holes had been gouged into the ground. I walked across the field to where the statues had been. Maren was at the makeshift desk, but she was slumped forward. I placed my hand gently on her shoulder.

Her eyes shot open in surprise, but when she saw it was me, she smiled.

"You never came back to the room, did you?"

"No," she admitted. "I got the baron to help me requisition the ingredients I needed for the elixir from some of the market vendors. They weren't happy about being awakened in the middle of the night, but the baron's gold eased their misgivings."

"I'm sure it did." I looked at the statues. There were over a dozen of them. "Have you tried the elixir yet?"

"Somewhat," Maren replied. "Since they are statues, I'm not sure how to administer it. I've tried pouring it on them, but that hasn't worked."

I remembered something Bekim had mentioned. "Have you tried waving it under their noses?"

Maren's face creased into an odd expression. "What?"

"Bekim said that when he was under the control of the sorcerer, he could still hear and see. I know being turned to stone is different, but it's still a form of magic, isn't it? Maybe they still have some of their senses."

Maren frowned. "It's a long shot, but I suppose it's worth trying."

She picked up a glass vial from the desk. The liquid inside was bright red, like blood. Maren walked over to one of the statues and held the vial under its nose. It was a young boy, roughly around Bekim's age as far as I could tell. She held it there for a long moment, then withdrew it. We waited. And waited.

Nothing happened.

14

"Well, it was worth trying." I heaved a sigh.

"Perhaps we can try soaking them in the potion," Maren suggested.

"Do you have enough to do that?"

"Possibly. I've got plenty of ingredients." Maren waved toward the desk and I saw a dozen cases stacked next to it. Leafy green vines overflowed from the top of one of them.

"What can I do to help?" I asked.

Before Maren could reply, an unusual noise caused us both to look at the statue. I stared intently, but there was only silence. Perhaps I'd been hearing things.

"You heard that, didn't you?" Maren asked.

Perhaps not. I nodded mutely. And then the noise happened again. I leaned in close and turned my left ear toward the statue. It sounded like someone was speaking, but it was muffled and the words weren't clear.

"I think he's trying to say something."

I looked at the statue's lips. They weren't moving, but a crack had appeared in the stone. I placed my finger gently on the crack and a few chips fell off. The crack grew, arcing out in several directions. A loud shattering sound filled the air, and the stone splintered. The pieces fell off the boy and he coughed, a puff of gray dust expelling from his mouth.

"It worked," Maren said, her tone a mix of relief and incredulity. "I was starting to think he'd lied."

"Are you all right?" I asked the boy.

He blinked slowly numerous times, then opened his mouth. "I … can't … move," he said, each word a struggle to get out.

"The potion," I said. "Pour it into his mouth."

Maren pressed the vial to his lips and lifted it gradually until the entirety of the liquid was gone. Seconds passed, then minutes. The first thing I noticed was that the boy's complexion got darker. And then his fingers moved, then his hands. He turned his head from side to side, and then took a step forward.

"Am I dead?" he asked, looking at me curiously.

"Not even close," I replied.

Maren took him by the hand and pulled him away from the debris that had fallen off his body and began brushing his clothes off. There were two more vials of the elixir on the desk, and I grabbed one and used it to restore Aria next. I followed the same steps, holding the vial under her nose and then pouring the liquid into her mouth once the stone had cracked.

She recovered more quickly than the boy, and I guessed that he'd probably been turned to stone before her. Maren made more of the elixir and I administered it, working my way through the line of statues until they were all alive again.

The baron and a retinue of his guards arrived, and Aria rushed to him, wrapping him in a hug. As the healing properties of the elixir took effect, the children left the arena to return to their homes. Gregor thanked us profusely and the baron told him to take a few days off to recuperate. He sent Aria to the castle with one of his guards, and then the only ones who remained were Giffor and his remaining guards, Maren, and myself. The baron looked around the arena, noting the mess of stone shards that littered the ground.

"I'll admit, I had my doubts about the two of you when you arrived. I thought Master Anesko was either a fool for sending you, or he was trying to intentionally offend me."

I saw Maren's expression turn dark, but the baron continued talking.

"Now I know that it was neither. You're both capable, if a bit rough around the edges. I'm a man of my word. You found Aria and returned her to me, and so I will not tell the king about your transgression."

"Thank you," I said.

Giffor waved his hand as if slapping my words away. "I'll be sure to express my gratitude to Master Anesko."

"What of the sorcerer?" Maren asked. "What

will you do with him?"

"I had his tongue removed so that he can't cast any spells," Giffor answered. "And he's been locked in the dungeon. He'll spend the rest of his miserable life down there, and considering how young he is, he will have plenty of time to consider his mistakes."

"We know that they were selling the statues, but we don't know who bought them or how many others are out there," Maren said. "I wish there was something more we could do."

"I've already thought about that," Giffor said. "I've asked Osvald to oversee a detailed search of the city to find the statues that were placed at people's homes. The sorcerer refused to say why they returned some of the children, but I suppose that's not important. Now that we have the elixir, we'll set things right."

"The remaining vials are there," Maren said, pointing to the desk.

"I'll have my soldiers collect them. You're welcome to stay at the castle as long as you need to, but I'm sure you're needed back at the Citadel."

Maren nodded. "Yes, I'm sure we are. We were supposed to check in with Master Anesko, but none of my messages were able to get through. I'm sure he's curious to know what's transpired."

"Very well. Thank you both, again. You've done Tiradale a great service."

Maren and I didn't bother returning to the

castle. We were wearing everything we'd brought with us, so we went straight to the stable. Sion was back to normal again, and she nuzzled me with her massive head as she stepped out of her stall.

I challenged Demris to a race back to the Citadel, she said.

Oh? I'm sure he'll enjoy that.

His pride will be the reason I beat him.

I looked at Maren. "I hope you're ready to lose," I said. "Sion's going to best Demris today."

Maren laughed obnoxiously loud, exaggerating her mirth. "That's hilarious," she said. "I don't want to hear you crying again when we leave you in the dust."

I mounted Sion and waited for Maren to get settled in her saddle. Sion and Demris exchanged looks, then they leaped into the air at the same time, their powerful wings stirring up dust below us. They kept pace with each other for a long while, but eventually, Demris took the lead. When Sion and I returned to the Citadel, Maren was waiting in the underground stable, her arms crossed over her chest as she leaned against Demris's shoulder.

"I can see the tears in your eyes from here," she joked.

"Sure you can," I replied, removing Sion's saddle. She stretched and curled up in her cave, and Maren and I entered the school. We tracked down Master Anesko to let him know we were back, and he asked us to write up a full report of the events at

Tiradale and meet him in his office chambers.

Maren offered to write the report. My handwriting was usually a sloppy mess, so I gladly allowed her to. Once we finished, we stopped by the dining hall to check for leftovers, then headed to Anesko's chamber.

I occupied myself by cleaning the dirt from under my nails while he read over the report. He paused a few times to ask questions, and Maren provided the answers. He finished reading and set the report aside.

"Why didn't you send me updates?" he asked. "Eldwin, I asked you to make sure she did so."

"I tried," Maren said. "I think there were disruptions with the magic caused by the sorcerer."

"I also think that's what made the dragons ill," I added. "Once he was dealt with, Sion returned to normal."

Anesko nodded, but there was something about his expression that bothered me. I don't think he doubted what we said, but maybe he knew something we didn't.

"Take a day or two to rest," he said. "I have another task for you two, and since you handled the baron so well, this one should be easy."

"What is it?" Maren asked.

"We can discuss it once you've gotten some rest."

Maren huffed. "You can't leave us in suspense

like this. It isn't fair."

Anesko glanced at me and I shrugged.

"Have it your way, then," he said. "Those rumors about—"

"Goblins?" Maren asked excitedly. "Is it the goblins?"

"Yes," Anesko confirmed, shaking his head. "We've received more reports of goblin sightings near the mountains. I'd like you to check into it."

Maren looked at me, a huge grin stretching her lips. "I told you we'd get to see goblins."

I groaned inwardly. There would be no talking her out of this one.

THE END

ABOUT THE AUTHOR

Richard Fierce is a fantasy and space opera author. He's been writing since childhood, but began publishing in 2007. Since then, he's written multiple novels and short stories.

In 2000, Richard won Poet of the Year for his poem *The Darkness*. He's also one of the creative brains behind the Allatoona Book Festival, a literary event in Acworth, Georgia.

A recovering retail worker, he now works in the tech industry when he's not busy writing.

He's married and has three step-daughters (pray for him), three dogs (huskies!), three cats, two ferrets and a fish. He basically has a zoo.

His love affair with fantasy was born in high school when a friend's mother gave him a copy of *Dragons of Spring Dawning* by Margaret Weis and Tracy Hickman.